Lukas Allonby is a university graduate with a love for the fantasy genre. From a young age, he has been writing, from short stories to novellas he loves to explore horror, science fiction and the fantasy world of storytelling. One of his favourite authors is the infamous Stephen King and he enjoys reading his work new and old, he draws a lot of his creative ideas from King's books and films adapted from his books like *The Shining* and *Pet Sematary*. In Lukas' spare time, he likes to hike up mountains with his little sandy dachshund to collect ideas for his next piece of writing.

This is for my family, for always standing by me and believing in me. This work would not be possible if not for your unwavering support.

Lukas Allonby

BITE IN THE NITE

AUSTIN MACAULEY PUBLISHERS™
LONDON • CAMBRIDGE • NEW YORK • SHARJAH

Copyright © Lukas Allonby 2024

The right of Lukas Allonby to be identified as author of this work has been asserted by the author in accordance with sections 77 and 78 of the Copyright, Designs and Patents Act 1988.

All rights reserved. No part of this publication may be reproduced, stored in a retrieval system, or transmitted in any form or by any means, electronic, mechanical, photocopying, recording, or otherwise, without the prior permission of the publishers.

Any person who commits any unauthorised act in relation to this publication may be liable to criminal prosecution and civil claims for damages.

This is a work of fiction. Names, characters, businesses, places, events, locales, and incidents are either the products of the author's imagination or used in a fictitious manner. Any resemblance to actual persons, living or dead, or actual events is purely coincidental.

A CIP catalogue record for this title is available from the British Library.

ISBN 9781035838875 (Paperback)
ISBN 9781035838882 (ePub e-book)

www.austinmacauley.com

First Published 2024
Austin Macauley Publishers Ltd®
1 Canada Square
Canary Wharf
London
E14 5AA

This is for my sister who inspires me to live as my authentic self.
My mum, who has always shown her undying support in everything I do.
This book would not be possible if not for your unwavering support.
Also thank you to Austin Macauley Publishers for believing in my book and making a dream come to life.

Synopsis

Can they escape the grip of this creature of the night?

Caleb is an 18-year-old living in a small town in Washington. In 1989, when he meets a girl called Ebony, they start a romantic relationship, but does he really know who he is getting into bed with? They go away to try and escape a stranger who is following them until he catches up with them. They are taken through a portal into another dimension where they come under attack by enemy forces – creatures much more powerful than themselves.

Chapter 1

It was dark under the shadow of the moon…the boy was running through the gloomy woods, rapidly engulfing him in their impenetrable trees. As he frantically tried to escape his pursuer, he got the sinking feeling that something was closing in on him. The forest was a dark blur full of unhappy shadows, and bushes that sat below his feet making him feel like he was running on air. He could smell something that smells like rotting flesh all around him, and the stench was so rancid that it felt like it was burning the hairs in his nose. How could something smell so bad? He had never smelt something so horrific in his life, and he had to struggle to keep the contents of his stomach inside. He was mid sprint when he quickly lost his footing, and was thrown down into the muddy ground hitting his face on a big rock as he crashed landed. He woke up dazed with a thumping pain in his head, and as he lifted his hand to touch it; he noticed the thick stream of blood flowing down his face from the chunk of flesh that had been ripped from his head. He tried to sit up, but the canopy above started spinning, and he immediately turned to the side and began violently heaving. Concussion. As he lay there silently trying to regain control of himself, he heard a twig snap in-front of where he lay; he froze to the spot. His heartbeat began racing at the speed of light, and he couldn't stop shaking with absolute terror. Something came into his field of view; it looked like a man. He wore a black suit and nothing on his feet; his long oily hair was pushed back out of his eyes so he could see better. He looked down at the man's hands and what he saw petrified him; long thin tendrils for fingers and yellow fingernails stained with blood. The attacker turned his head suddenly, and lifted his hands slowly as if reaching into the air to grab him. Within seconds, the stranger was inches from his face and with a garish crunch and a gut churning splat; the boy's head was now eyeless as the stranger pulled his fingers out of the sockets, and the eyeballs slipped to the floor. The man placed his hands gently to the boy's neck and slashed effortlessly, and blood began spurting out of the incision. The man leant down towards the neck of his victim where there was a stream of pure blood gushing out of the wound, and sank his pointy fangs in…sucking on and devouring the blood. Vampires had returned to town.

TODAY – It was a dull rainy day in the small town of Forest Grove – Washington, and Caleb had just finished his daily swim. He was used to the wet weather because it never stopped raining, but he didn't mind because he loved the water. A thick fog lined the soaring trees around him, and dragons-breath brushed past his lips ferociously every time breathed out. He was walking home on the side of the highway when he saw a fancy car drive past with the windows blacked out. He thought this was strange as no one had fancy cars in Forest Grove. Caleb was a 6'1" 18-year-old with dark brown hair and blue eyes. He had a muscular physique and was a popular boy in high school. He had only one serious girlfriend ever and that ended badly; she had broken his heart and moved away suddenly, and ever since then, he had kept to himself. Caleb liked to think that he was over his ex, but there were times when he lay awake at night, thinking about her and all the things they had planned to do together. Do you ever really get over your first love? As he approached the two-floor house he lived in with his mum and his dog Percy; he felt a presence surrounding him. He looked to the left at the house next door which had recently been sold, and he recognised the fancy car he saw on the highway earlier. Were they his new neighbours? Something in the top window of the house caught his eye; someone behind the curtain was watching him with beady eyes. He shook the peculiar feeling off and opened the front door to his house; he was greeted by a sloppy kiss from Percy, his relentless Sandy coloured Doberman. He called out to his mum, but she wasn't in; she must have been working. He let the dog out the backdoor into the huge backyard that overlooked a small lake that sat behind the row of houses. The fog sat on the surface of the lake creating an eerie presence, like something was ready to emerge from the depths of it and swallow you whole. Caleb called the dog back in and closed the door behind him, making sure to lock the door.

Ebony was tired of constantly moving from place to place – it made it impossible to settle down with someone or even make friends. She never had a sense of belonging, and it left a vast emptiness within her. She was incredibly beautiful with her long blonde hair flowing, and when she had it tied up in a messy bun, her big blue eyes looked as though they were oceans deep and anyone who looked in them for too long would risk drowning in them. Although she looked like a goddess on the outside, there was a darkness that sat just below the surface; every now and then, after spending time with her family, she felt herself falling back into the abyss. There was a reason they always moved around, and it was her fault because she was the one who caused the accident, well the sort of accident. She didn't mean to kill that man. She and her family had been running from the past for years, and that's why they never settled down in one place; she was miserable! She had hoped that this town would be different, that maybe she could fit in somewhere for once. It was raining when the family car drove down an unfamiliar highway, and she was looking out of the window at the gloomy fog blanketing the thick pine trees. She was almost daydreaming when she suddenly caught sight of a tall figure walking down the sidewalk ahead. She perked up as she drove past so she could get a better look at the person, and she was shocked to see that this boy was incredibly beautiful; he was tall, tanned, and muscular, and he had sadness in his face, and Ebony felt like she could relate. As they drove away into the distance; she caught herself looking back at the boy with a sense of longing. The car pulled up to the only house with a for sale sign in the front yard, and as the engine cut off, she opened the car door, swung her legs out and jumped down quickly. She looked around at her surroundings. The houses were huge, and they all looked like they had been built recently – modern. They were tall and seemed to be made with a light colour brick; black roofs and black doors creating a shadow over the street. Each long paved drive had a big expensive car, some even had two – she was in the rich part of town. Once they had unloaded the car and settled into the house, she walked up the marble staircase and into her new bedroom. It was spacious with a double bed and a big wardrobe, and she had her own bathroom so she could shower at 1 am when she was having an episode and not disturb anyone. She was messing with her black silk curtains when she heard someone walking up the path next-door; she sneaked a peak around the blind and saw the boy she had seen walking on the sidewalk. Could he really live next door to me? Was this fate at work? The boy looked suddenly up at her bedroom window and she had to quickly dive away towards the ground. As she landed in a heap on the floor, she prayed to God that he didn't see her.

Chapter 2

It had been two days since his new mysterious neighbour had moved in, and they were yet to meet. Like usual, it was a dull foggy morning, and after he showered and ate his breakfast, he got Percy on his lead and headed out back towards the quaint little lake. It was chilly, and goosebumps started to form up and down his body, making him shiver uncontrollably. He was walking into the thick of the trees now, and something in him told him to turn around and check if anything was behind him... nothing. He carried on marching into the distance while throwing a stick for the dog to chase. After a while, Caleb got tired and sat down on a big grey rock surrounded by thick green bushes; it was silent up here apart from the birds whistling above him; this was the only place he felt true peace. He heard something in the distance, like branches snapping underfoot – someone was walking towards him. The wind started to pick up – howling like a wolf on a full moon; he stood up and looked around, trying to see what or who the noise was coming from. In the distance, he could see a figure begin to come into focus, and as it got closer, he could make out the distinctive facial features of a woman. She had the most striking eyes, as though oceans were storming around in them, and the way she walked was like she was floating, so graceful in her stride. As she made her way to stand in front of Caleb, he found himself lost for words at her sheer beauty. She began to open her mouth as if to speak, but nothing came out, or was Caleb unable to hear now? He closed his eyes tight and took several deep breaths in and out to settle his nerves, and when he opened his eyes, he was alone and the dog was barking at him. Where was the girl? Was she ever there or did he just imagine her? If he did imagine it, then what did this mean for him, was he going crazy? He got up and whistled to Percy; he set off back down the path that led back to his house with the big stick in his hand making sure the dog was close by; he didn't feel safe anymore. When he got back into his house, he went straight up to his bedroom and threw himself down onto the bed in heap intent on falling asleep.

He was falling in and out of consciousness, and he was having a bad dream. In this dream, he was being chased by something and he didn't know what it was. All he knew was that he had to get away before it got to him. He was running through the woods, and the moon was shining bright above the tall trees; the wind was smacking him hard in the face as he tried to run against it. He was scrambling his way along the wooded floor when his foot got caught in a web of thorns that viciously ripped into his flesh. He cried out in agony as the thorns unleashed their poison into his bloodstream; his body started to tremble uncontrollably and he could feel himself beginning to faint from the pain. He woke up in a puddle of sweat in the middle of his bed, and a gust of wind hit him in the face, his window was open.

He quickly jumped up and ran to the window, the window wasn't open when he fell asleep, so who or what had opened it? He went downstairs and started calling for his mum, but when he couldn't find her, he started to panic; someone must have been in the house and they could still be IN the house. He got his bat from under the stairs and called for Percy, but he didn't come. He shouted again for his dog to come, but he was nowhere to be seen; he walked into the kitchen and saw that back door standing A-jar and his heart sank. He immediately thought that Percy had escaped and ran away, but when he stepped out into the cold night, he saw that he was sitting in the yard with the girl he thought he saw earlier on the trail. She was as beautiful as she was when he first saw her, and as he walked down to the yard, she looked up at him with her ocean eyes.

"Hi, I hope you don't mind me stroking your dog," said the girl.

"Hey, it's okay, he doesn't usually like strangers," Caleb replied.

"I'm Ebony, I moved next door yesterday."

"I thought I saw you; I'm Caleb, it's nice to meet you."

Do you believe in love at first sight? In that moment, right then, Caleb fell in love. Something about her voice, a soft velvety lullaby playing on repeat in his head felt like heaven. When he thought of her, he forgot about all of his problems, and although he had only just met her, he had a deep feeling that this was only the beginning.

Chapter 3

Ebony was in her room watching the television when she suddenly began to feel a sickly feeling making its way up her oesophagus. She knew what this meant as soon as it started to happen, and she quickly dashed to the bathroom. She made it to the toilet on time, and after she had finished bringing her insides up, she was still on the bathroom floor. This happened every time she thought about the thing. You see, there was a reason why they constantly moved around; there was a sickness in Ebony that was incurable, and it made her act crazy. When she lived in upstate New York, something bad happened; she was walking home to her apartment complex she shared with her friend at the time, and she had been reading about a string of grisly murders occurred near where she lived. They weren't normal murders. They were heinous, ghastly acts committed by a real psychopath. Limbs were missing and the eyeballs of some of the victims were taken out and placed next to the bodies; some were missing their heads and some were fully clothed, and others completely stark naked. She was used to watching horror movies and murder documentaries, so the gore didn't really bother her. It was a glum day, and the clouds were as dark as the deep sea, murky. The smog was subsiding as she walked into it, forming a trail for her. She started to see blue lights forming on the horizon, but this wasn't anything new. A loud clap of thunder broke out above her, and the rain started to come down heavily, streaming down her face as though she was crying a river. A peculiar squeal echoed just up the street from her, and as it intertwined with the wind it penetrated every fissure in her body. She wiped the moisture from her face, and as she pulled her hand away from her face she saw a red splodge on her hand; she blinked hard, but it was still there when she opened them again. She looked down at her white t-shirt and she saw blood-splattered stains all over her, hands saturated with thick sticky plasma. She was alarmed and suddenly breathing was difficult for Ebony; she fell against a wall and had to compose herself. What had she done? She quickly ran down a back street away from the lights of main street, and began to take her clothes off; she had to get rid of the evidence. She ripped off her white t-shirt and began to scrub her hands violently. There was a deep puddle on the ground, and she got down onto her knees and doused her hands in the water. It was cold, so cold it was freezing her veins. After she had done this, she stood up unsteadily and walked back towards the main street; now she was half-naked and shivering. She looked left and right, and then suddenly started running fleetingly to her apartment, avoiding eye contact with the strangers she passed on the way. The people of New York were probably accustomed to seeing a crazy half naked woman running up the street, probably high on some drug. When she got back to her apartment, she unlocked it with shaky hands and burst the door open when she heard the key click in the lock. She scampered to the bathroom as quickly as she could and began forcefully retching.

She remembered it all, the strangulation, the dismemberment, it all came rushing back. The splitting of the flesh as it came apart from the bone, and the gnawing of the bone as it connected with the meat cleaver. She remembered feeling a nagging sensation in her gut when she committed that first murder, but at the same time, she felt empowered and invigorated. She recalled finding him on the docks just down the road from her apartment complex; she lay in weight behind some shipping containers out of the way so no one could see her. She spotted him walking slowly down the embankment, stumbling all over the place. She moved from my position quietly, like a mouse, she tiptoed behind him for about half a mile, and then suddenly she hurled herself at him like a lion pouncing on its prey. She seized his neck and opened her mouth wide, and these long white shark-like fangs protruded from mouth. She sank them ferociously into the man's neck, and sucked the life right out of him. The man was crying for help, but each cry was cut off by the crashing of the waves against the dock wall. He lost consciousness and sagged to the floor; after she had done draining him; she snapped his neck to make sure he was dead. She had to get rid of the body; first, she dragged him to a boatshed that had been left unlocked, and placed him on a tarp lying on the floor. She took his boots off first and placed them on the side; she then took his pants and his shirt off, and did the same thing. She grabbed the meat cleaver and cut through his flesh like he was a joint of beef. Tender blood and puss oozing out of the open abrasions. Everything was going okay until she got to the bone; she found it difficult to cut through the bone. I applied pressure as I hacked down onto the bone, and this time, the bone cracked and crumbled away; a sigh of relief escaped from her mouth as she continued. She had removed both arms and one leg; all she had to do now was remove the other leg and take the head. She looked intently at his lifeless face; his blue eyes richer than any sea staring back at her equally blue eyes, almost making her feel remorse for taking such beautiful eyes away from the world. She ran her hands over the bite marks on his neck and traced his face with her thumb. She grabbed the pen knife from her pocket, and carved her initial into his cheek, her mark. She ripped his head off his shoulders, the skin tearing and dangling off the open bone. The head got wrapped in the clothes that had been taken away from the victim and once she had removed all the bits of the body; she gathered them all together and threw them into the water in different directions. Scattered, torn to pieces, she disappeared back to the safety of her apartment.

Chapter 4

When Ebony woke on the bathroom floor the next morning, she felt groggy. The flashback had followed her into her dreams, and all she could think about was the murder. She didn't want to be like this; she asked herself why she was like this, couldn't she be a good vampire? A vampire that doesn't hunt humans. She got in the shower and washed all the regret off her, it followed her around like a blanket clinging to her body. It was a bright sunny day and the light was creeping in through the blinds, creating a warm sensation on her skin. The reason she could stand in the sun without combusting was a necklace she wore around her neck; it protected her from the sun and anything that would try to harm her; her mother gave it to her when she turned. Of course, there had been more than one instance where she needed to be protected, but it didn't protect her from wanting to kill people, like the man she killed in New York. She had lost count of how many people she had murdered and mutilated, but no matter how hard she tried to stop, she could not resist. She wanted to know the boy next door, but she was worried she would end up killing him, so she got dressed and threw some makeup on quickly. She grabbed an apple and headed out of the door without looking back. It was a Saturday, so he must have been at home, where else could he have been? She walked across the freshly mowed lawn and over the newly planted rose bushes and onto the driveway of the boy next door. She was nervous to see him again, but she wanted to know him better, so she looked at the doorbell and pressed it twice. She could hear banging around in the house, and then the door opened wide and out came Caleb, dressed in gym gear looking very tired, but handsome. They looked at each other for a while before either one said anything, which was slightly awkward, so eventually, she took one for the team.

"Hey, I hope I'm not intruding, have you got time to talk?" Ebony asked.

"I was just headed out to the gym; can I catch you later? I'll give you my number and I'll call you when I'm home," he replied quickly.

He took my phone from me and began typing his number in; when he was done, he handed it back to me and smiled; it was a beautiful smile. She suddenly felt her heart begin to race; her skin felt like sandpaper rubbing against her veins, she needed to feed. They said goodbye, and then Ebony turned back towards her house, but this time she went down the side of the house towards the back garden gate at the bottom of the garden near the little lake. Maybe she could find someone who was hiking alone up the path of the forest; it was dangerous, and she could easily get caught in this small town, but if this were what would stop her from harming him, she would do it. It was cold and crispy, and when she breathed out, she had dragons' breath that poured out in front of her; as she walked out onto the forest path, she looked around at the scenery; the sky was bright blue and the sun was rising towards its highest peak shining bright, creating some form of heat that was warm when it touched her skin. The birds were singing songs in the trees and darting from one to the other, and the smell of the fresh air running through her nostrils and deep into her lungs made her feel like she was alive. She could see, hear, and smell things more vividly because she was a vampire; she could hear someone walking miles away; she could smell blood, and she could hear screams and cries much more clearly than a human could. She stalked up the path slowly so she could enjoy the day and relax, and as she was walking, she could hear footsteps ahead round a bend in the trees; she ducked down behind a big rock and watched to see if this could be potential fuel for her. As she laid in wait, she saw a woman in full hiking gear walking down towards her; she looked like she was alone. Ebony got ready to pounce on the lone woman 3...2...1, JUMP. She collided with the woman, and they both fell onto the ground in a heap. The hiker was pinned to the ground by Ebony's strong arms, and there was no escaping her tight grip. Ebony pulled her head up and bared her pointy teeth, and then she sunk them deeply into the woman's carotid artery; blood came squirting out of the puncture wound and into the mouth of the vampire. The sensation she felt when the blood flowed down her throat was almost orgasmic; in the moment, her whole body was taken over. It was like an out-of-body experience. Then suddenly, it was over and she was left in the forest alone, leaning over a corpse. Now that all the excitement was over and she was feeling less on edge, she had to get rid of the body; she picked the woman up and dragged her back down the path all the way to her back garden. When she got to the back gate of her house, she dropped the body before going inside and looking around to see if anyone was watching her. The coast was clear, so she pulled the body into the house and into the bathroom, and while she ran the bath, she started taking off the clothes of the woman. Once she had run the bath with cold water, she plunged the body in the water to make it easier to carve her up. She pushed her head under the water, and bobbed up and down for a while, and then Ebony found a sponge and started to caress the victim's face with it gently until she grabbed a knife and began to carve her face up like a joint of meat. She cut the tongue off and blood began to drip incessantly, so she placed it in her mouth and sucked the tongue until it was bone dry. Blood was dripping down her chin and onto the bathroom floor, saturating the bathmat; she tossed the tongue aside and turned her focus to the lifeless body floating in front of her. She went and retrieved an axe from another room which she used to dismember the head of the woman, and before she cut the head off, she carved her initial into the cheek of the head to make sure her mark was left. She used a bone saw to cut the other limbs off, and while she did this in the bath, the bath water turned a bright red colour. Once she had only a torso left in the tub, she emptied the bath and filled it up with acid, so she could throw the limbs in there and leave no trace. By the time there were only bones left in the tub; she looked up and saw that the walls surrounding her were covered with blood, and bits of disregarded flesh were seen littered all over the place. She began bleaching the tub and cleaning the walls; the smell of bleach was burning her eyes, making them water. She collected everything from the bathroom including the severed head she kept as a souvenir and moved into her bedroom. She set everything down and started to pull up one of her floorboards; after she did this, she grabbed the head and the left-over bones and placed them gently into the floor. The floorboard was placed back into position, and then she went back into the bathroom and took a shower, ready to meet up with Caleb.

Chapter 5

Caleb had texted Ebony the night he had got back from the gym, and she had come over after he had showered. At first, he felt awkward because they had only just met, but after some time, it felt natural. She was the most beautiful girl he had ever seen. When she spoke, he hung onto every single word she said, and they spoke for hours about anything and everything. When it came to saying goodnight, they got closer to each other and Caleb wanted to kiss her. He made his move and it turned out she wanted to kiss him too. They stayed in this position, intertwining themselves together. Caleb opened his eyes and screamed; Ebony's face had changed; her eyes were all bloodshot and red, and when she opened her mouth, she had teeth as sharp as razors. He stumbled back and cried out.

"What ARE you?" he screamed at her.

She started to back away feeling at her face. She had nearly lost control of herself, and now he knew her secret. She was going to have to kill him.

"Please calm down," she begged.

Caleb tried to escape through the window because the door was blocked, but she got there first and grabbed him. She pinned him down onto the floor and began to answer his question; she told him she was a vampire. At first, he didn't believe her because who would? Vampires don't exist because they're a fairy tale, just like witches and werewolves are. It took several hours for him to come around from receiving this information, but when he did, he wasn't scared; for some reason, he felt safe with her. Once everything had calmed down, they said goodbye and Caleb went into the bathroom. He looked at himself in the mirror; he looked tired and ill, but he never felt more alive. He got into bed and fell asleep almost instantly.

When he dreamt that night, he dreamt only of Ebony; her blonde hair flowing down all over him, and her blue eyes meeting his eyes creating an intense desire to tear their clothes off. He woke suddenly in a puddle of sweat, but not from a nightmare. He couldn't wait to text her, and he snatched his phone up from his bed quickly and began to type a message, but before he could finish, he heard a whirring sound behind him, and there standing before him was Ebony.

"I was just about to text you," he said.

"I was waiting until you were awake to come in." she replied.

"Wait...how did you know I was awake?" he asked.

"It's a secret," she winked.

Both decided to go into town that day. On the way into the quaint little town, they walked past several cute little cottages that had smoke coming out of the chimneys and small doors and windows like a house fit for an elf. Ebony had never seen anything like this; she was used to moving around different cities bustling with life. It was so quiet here. There were only a couple of cars and one wagon that rushed past them as they walked along the almost desolate highway. It was starting to rain lightly as they got into town so they ran into the local bookshop for shelter. The walls were lined with a multitude of different books, Stephen King, children's books, thrillers, and more. The smell in there was strong; a strong book smell wafting up their nostrils mixed with the moisture on their clothes from the dew outside. They walked to the back of the shop and found a section to sit down and read a book in; they sat down and began to talk some more. Over the past few days, they had done a lot of talking and getting to know each other, and Caleb wasn't even scared of her. Maybe this could work for her. As the day flew by, they were both too caught up in each other to see that it was nearly nightfall, and they would have to walk home in the dark.

They both got up and left the store and as they started to walk home, Ebony decided to walk in the direction of the forest path. The darkness was all around her trying to suffocate them both. He followed her like a lost puppy into the unknown ahead of them. It was calm at night; there were no people out here so they could be whatever they want without having to hide. Ebony had an idea in her head. She wanted to share immortality with Caleb; even though it had only been a few days, she knew she wanted him to be with her forever. As they got deeper into the gulf of darkness, they stopped in a shallow clearing, a dip in the woods hidden from the naked eye. It was easy to turn someone into a vampire. All you had to do was feed on them to the point of death, and right at the last second, drop a pinch of the vampire blood into their mouth. Only a drop was needed to turn someone. She grabbed him by the scruff of the neck in a passionate way, and before he knew what was happening, he was on the floor and she was shredding his neck open and devouring the blood that was dispensing out of his neck at a fast rate. Caleb was in and out of consciousness and didn't know what was happening until he felt something dripping into his mouth. It tasted sour. There was a moment where everything stood still; time and space was stopped in its tracks. Suddenly Caleb cried out in sheer pain; his gums were burning like there was something under them trying to get out. His blood began to race through his veins at high speed, and his muscles were clenching up. He finally came around to normality, and his first thought was blood. He wanted blood.

Chapter 6

2 DAYS LATER

She woke up in her bed. The bright light was shining through her blinds.

"Oh crap, the light!" She said out loud.

Caleb was hiding behind his wardrobe because the light was burning the flesh from his bones; was this a side-effect of being a vampire, and what the hell was he going to do about it? He turned around and there she stood, holding out a ring for him. The ring was big and bulky, but it was a beautiful orange colour.

"Quick, put this on, it will protect you," shouted Ebony as she tossed the ring across the room. He dashed to put in on his finger, dropping it by mistake, accidentally placing his hand in direct sunlight, and crying out in agonising pain as the sun penetrated his skin follicles. They walked through the house and into the backyard towards the gate, and the lake. Once they arrived at the lake, they had the spontaneous idea to skinny dip; even though it wasn't the ocean, it was close enough. One by one, they started removing an item of clothing; first was the shoes, and then came the pants until the only thing left was their tops. They were naked as they dived into the cold lake. The water hit them like a ton of bricks immediately waking them up and if they were humans; they would have gone into shock, but they were much more powerful now. They swam down to the bottom, pulling the weight of their bodies down, fighting against the force of the water. They could see fish swimming around in the distance, but nothing bigger than a fish because it was only a small pond. Caleb longed to be in the open ocean, swimming with dolphins and hitching a ride on the back of a giant blue whale. The ocean was always a place of comfort for Caleb. He loved to be in the water; when he was younger, he used to think he was the son of Poseidon, the Greek God of the Sea. One thing he noticed was that he didn't need to come up to take a breath; now that he was technically dead, he could breathe like a fish. He felt like a fish in water, and his feet had morphed into a big fin. He looked to his left and saw that Ebony had a tail like a mermaid. Was it possible that all the mythological creatures you read about in books are real, or was he just hallucinating? They collided together in a passionate embrace of the water, circling around them until they were in their own private bubble; in this moment, they were one person moulded together by lust. They pushed their way to the surface and shed water for a while, still looking at each other intensely. They got out of the water and dried themselves off, and once they were dry, they decided they needed to feed on something, or someone. This was the first time that he fed; Ebony decided to teach him the best way to hunt prey. She took him to the very top of the trail where no one ever goes, so that they could see down from the top. As luck would have it, there were people walking near the top of the trail today; how unfortunate for them. They both led down in the tall grass, so they would not be seen; Caleb copied every move she took. She could hear the creaking trees swaying in the wind; the birds weren't chirping this high up, so the only thing she could hear other than the wind was the distant mumblings of the victims she prepared to slaughter. It was a couple, husband and wife, possibly. They stopped at the end of the trail and began to take their water bottles out for refreshment when the vampires took their chance to snatch them. It all happened very quickly; one minute, they were led in the grass watching, and the next, they were covered in blood and laying over the lifeless sacks of pork. It was exhilarating!

A few hours later, they had heaved the bodies back into the house of Ebony where they had to get rid of all traces of them. Caleb sat back and watched as she took all her tools out and laid them out in a specific order; she took the bone she saw first. She removed all the limbs like she usually did, but this time when she was done carving the corpse up, she didn't fill the bath up with acid to get rid of the flesh. Instead, she took a bite out of it and swallowed as though it was the nicest tasting roast chicken. She looked at him and passed him a piece of flesh, prompting him to eat it. This was entirely new to them; they had never eaten anybody before.

Chapter 7

It was early in the morning, about 7 am, and it was still dark out. The wolves were howling at the top of their lungs. All was quiet in the town that lay below the hilled mountain, but something was stirring in the bushes. It strolled out of the dimness wryly as though it was losing its balance. It was a man dressed in a black suit with his hair all greased back. His hands were long and pointy at the ends, and his eyes were red, like the devil. The grand high vampire had returned to collect his children. When you think of a head vampire, you think of Dracula or Nosferatu, but that is nothing but fairy tale; the reality is much scarier. He was much stronger than the other vampires, so much so that he didn't need a necklace or a ring to protect him from the sunlight; the only thing that stopped him from going into the sunlight was the fact that his skin changed colour when it was in contact with the sunlight. A few days ago, he had the burning desire to come to this little town on the coast of Oregon. Something inside of him was telling him that he needed to come and collect something. When he arrived, he stalked around the woods for a while, looking for a bite when he came across two young teenagers feeding on two other humans. He found this curious because he had finally found what he was looking for, two little vampire children. He held back and watched them as they dragged the bodies down the hill and back to the residence. He had waited long enough; he had to go and find them before they fed again and risked exposing the vampire species.

He had reached the bottom of the path and was looking directly into the windows of the children; one light was on and the other was off; could they have been together? He was just about to turn around and go back into hiding when the curtain behind one of the windows started to move like someone was behind it. He kept his stare on the window for a few minutes, but no further activity occurred, so he went back into the abyss.

Ebony was sure that someone was watching her; she could feel it on her skin; she lightly moved the curtain to the side so she could see outside into the world, and she thought she saw something sitting on the edge of the forest, but she couldn't be sure because it was wearing all black, the only visible thing was his icy pale skin. She quickly backed away, hoping that she wasn't seen, and immediately started to get dressed to go over to Caleb's house.

When she arrived, he was already dressed and awake, pacing around his bedroom so fast it was hard to see him clearly.

"What is wrong with you?" she asked concerningly.

"Did you see it, that thing in the woods?" he replied hastily.

"I mean yeah, but I couldn't make out what it was; it was too dark."

"It was a man in a black suit, he was sitting there watching us, and when I looked at him, I felt a connection to him."

They conversed about this for a while and eventually agreed that they should leave town for a while, and get a little cabin on the beach out of the way for a while. They went their separate ways to start packing a bag quickly; they decided they could walk to the cabin on the beach because it wasn't too far away that they needed a car. They would sneak out the front of their houses, making sure to not be seen by anyone, and then they would join the wooded path on the other side of the road that, if followed, led to the sandy beach. They met there at 3 pm sharp; it was a workday, so the children were at work and the adults were at work, so the roads were quiet, quieter than usual. They held hands as they crossed the road, discreetly looking around for eyes peeping out of the green and brown canopies. They crept like a thief in the night, and once they had escaped into the distance, they relaxed a little. After walking for about an hour, they reached the orange sandy beach; the smell of the ocean rich in the air. The spray off the sea catching a ride on the wind and smashing into their faces. Ocean breeze. They got to the cabin and entered through the little wooden door, locked shut behind them. As soon as he dropped his bags, he slammed the blinds shut to protect them from any unwanted visitors. When they looked around, they could see a little kitchen area with a stove, an old fashioned kettle, pots of coffee and bags of tea. In the far end of the cabin was a mattress with a knitted blanket placed gently on top. They both went and sat down on the floor next to the bed, making little to no noise at all, so quiet you could hear a mouse scuttering on the roof of the cabin.

In the deep stirring darkness of the woods, he was lurking. The very powerful, blood-thirsty vampire was waiting for the young pair to evacuate their quaint little cabin before he made his move. It was proving much more difficult waiting to catch them. By now, they would have known who he was and what he looked like, but he didn't want to hurt them; he wanted to recruit them onto his team. But was his team good or evil? Did they mean well by exterminating the bad from the world? It could be argued that he believed he was a good vampire – if there was such a thing – but aren't vampires' children of the devil? He had a lot of vampires he recruited over the years of living in captivity; people he met along the way stayed loyal to him. Whenever he came across newborns, he tried recruiting them, to help them. He knew that this was going to be a difficult talk that could be dragged out a long time, weeks, months, and possibly years, depending on how long they ran from him.

Chapter 8

Daylight. Beaming light came in through a tiny gap; outside they could hear the ocean crashing against the shore. They could smell the beautiful fresh sea air seeping in through the cracks of the door. They looked at each other with a look of pure love, like they had never looked at anyone else before. It was quiet for a second, and this was when they heard the footsteps on the roof. They were too heavy to be the mouse running over it last night. Could it be a bigger mammal? Or was it the man hiding in the forest? He got up quickly and ran to the window where he sneakily peeked around the closed blind trying to see if he could see anything or anyone near them. It was blustery outside; not many people were out on the beach, but he did see a few stray dogs running on the beach, a few miles down the beach. He looked down to the stairs that led to the door of their cabin, and he could see a dark shadow forming on the steps, he pulled away discreetly.

"He is here. He has found us," he cried out.

"What, who?" she replied in a panic.

They began to run around the cabin in a fit of sheer panic. Grabbing hold of all their belongings and shoving them into a bag. The banging on the roof got loud until it wasn't on the roof anymore, but it was right outside the door. There were three loud knocks on the wooden door. Although they were only small knocks, they sent vibrations through the whole of the cabin, possibly the whole beach. In the space of a few seconds, the front of the cabin was ripped from the rest of the structure, pieces of splintered wood flying, and the ripping sound of the wood departing from the sandy ground. In the middle of the colossal mess was a man with long hair and a smart black suit; he was very pale and had bright red piercing eyes. A cunning smile formed across his face as he saw the faces of the two children in front of him drop to the ground, a crooked toothy smile.

"Hello children, I have been searching for you. I am Marcel, the Grand High Vampire of Brooklyn," said the man directly to the children.

"How did you find us?" Replied Caleb shakily.

"Are you going to hurt us?" asked Ebony.

"My dear, I do not intend on hurting you. I just want to take you in, train you, and teach you the proper ways of being an undead being. It seems you have been making a mess."

There was a sudden tingling feeling inside both children, a sort of warm feeling that told them that they could trust him. They walked swiftly behind him in silence looking down at their feet, holding each other's hands tightly, locking their sweaty fingers together. The man stopped walking and raised his hand to the side to stop them from walking any further. They looked up and saw that they were in the water – waist deep – but they weren't wet. They should have been soaking wet, but they were bone dry. It was like magic. They could feel the cold water splashing into them but their clothes were dry.

"How is this happening, we aren't getting wet?" asked Caleb curiously.

"This is the entrance to the portal. It's laced with magic so we can walk in; no human can find it because they cannot walk in the water without getting wet, so it's the perfect hiding place for a portal to another world," replied the Grand High Vampire of Brooklyn.

"Another world? How is this even possible? We can't leave our families behind," exclaimed Ebony.

Almost without hearing the children's complaints, he carried on moving forward, deeper into the ocean. They plodded on after him unsure as to why they were following his lead until eventually, a door with a big lock on was looming just in front of them. It was a large red door with a big gold lock in the middle; he stopped just and pulled out a rather large key from inside his suit pocket. The children wondered how he fit such a large key into such a small pocket, but they were distracted from that thought by the man inserting the key and turning it clockwise slowly over and over. It suddenly clicked, but the man hesitated, he slowly turned around and spoke to the children directly.

"What you are about to enter will change your thoughts on everything; you will see many different things that will blow your mind, you must not react."

This scared them. What more could they possibly find out that could be worse than being dead?

Chapter 9

The door began to lean open, and a blaring light began to poke through; it was electric blue and pink mixed together, shining bright like a diamond. They could hear distant screams even before they stepped through the portal, deathly yells, blood curdling screams. Caleb inched forward shuffling his feet, still holding Ebony's hand tightly as she followed his every move. All of them stepped through at the same time, and for a moment, it was pitch black; all colours had gone away and the only sound was the constant screaming. The reason that everything was black was because they had their eyes shut; once they opened their eyes, they were taken aback. It was like a whole new world, there was no limit on the sky. It was like they were looking straight up into outer space. There were a multitude of houses and creepy little shops; it was like it was a normal town but it was laced with vampires, dog-like creatures, peculiar old women dressed up in robes – perhaps witches and warlocks. They wore brown and purple robes, and eccentric pointy hats; I mean they knew that people practised witchcraft in that day and age, but these were actual witches who possessed magical powers. They could smell a bizarre odour; it was a mix of damp and mothballs, but then there was a hint of grass and flowers, depending on what you were looking at. If you looked at the nice little houses on the left, you could smell the flowers, but if you look at the dark looking houses and large intimidating apartments, you could smell the damp smell. There was a large contrast between the two sides, especially the people; the people seemed to match which side of town they came from. The creatures crawling out of the ground on the right side were some of the most horrifying things they had ever seen; some had giant green scabs all over them, and others were riddled with long black straw-like hair and talons for hands, like something straight out of the depths of Tartarus. If you looked out in the distance, you could see a faint red line which was confirmed by Marcel to be the entrance to their hell, filled with the souls of the eternally damned. This sent a shiver down the spines of the children. If these creatures in front of them weren't eternally damned, then what were the ones in 'their hell' going to look like? One thing that they noticed was the lack of transport; there were no vehicles of any sort, and they felt like they had been thrown back in time.

"Where are the cars?" asked Caleb.

"Cars haven't been invented here, there is no need for such things when we have magic," replied Marcel in a hushed voice.

Marcel began to walk down the grey cobbled street, intent on a house towards the bottom of the road. The children followed quickly, whilst taking in their surroundings and familiarising themselves with the folk emerging from the ground and various orifices. It was already quite obvious that these creatures were not humanoid, but sort of alien-like, a new species or a very old species possibly. They reached a bright orange door with a bunch of flowers at the doorstep, on the door read – Dora's witchcraft shack – this was the witch that would sort accommodation and clothing out for the children, but she was also Marcel's wife. When they entered the shop, they were surprised at how normal it seemed to look; there were bookshelves lining the wall with an array of different witch cookbooks; there were also books like Frankenstein and Dracula – which made it seem like a normal bookshop. When they moved towards the back of the shop, there was a curtain made from shells covering a hole in the back of the shop; when they walked through the shells, they banged back against their skin and punched them – Caleb cried out in pain and shock. What he saw on the other side of the curtain made him stand still; there was a beautiful woman with long dark hair and misty grey eyes piercing through his soul; Marcel bent down to where she was sitting and proceeded to kiss her on the mouth softly, like the leaves of a rose petal.

"Hello, I am Dora, and who are you?" she asked the two of them.

"Hhhii, my name's Ebony, and this is Caleb," Ebony replied shakily.

"These are the two children I was telling you about; they were very hard to find, but I managed to grab them and bring them here; could you help find them clothes and a bed darling?"

"Of course, just give me a minute."

After a few minutes, the witch took Ebony into a small room in the back and began to pick out clothes for her to wear. When she came back out of the room, she looked absolutely stunning in a black Lycra suit. She looked like a spy because her hair was up in a tight bun on her head; Caleb thought he couldn't fall in love anymore that he had, but he was so wrong. It was his turn now; she took him away into the room in the back and began to size him up with her beady little eyes. She reached out for a tape measure and began throwing it all over his body, taking measurements. When she had eventually finished, she pulled out a dark suit that was similar to that of Marcels; she pulled out some dark boots for him to wear that made him look like he was wearing moon boots. When he looked in the mirror, he liked what saw; he looked strong and his muscles were popping out of his new shirt. Since he has transformed into a vampire, he looked pale, but he also looked powerful and he liked this. He walked back into the front of the shop and he felt the silence as Marcel and Ebony were looking at him...no, not looking...staring.

He started to feel uncomfortable; he could feel his cheeks turning as red as a tomato. The silence was broken by Dora coming back into the room and telling them where they would be staying while they were there.

Chapter 10

They were walking up a hill towards a big house. It sat on top of the hill and looked down at everything below it, like a hawk looking down on its prey. Once they reached the bottom of the stairs, they paused and caught their breath. The house close-up was worse than it seemed at the bottom of the hill; it was a haunted mansion and the paint was crumbling off the outside; the wood on the porch wrapped around the house was eroding so much so that if they put their foot in the wrong place, they could fall straight through into hell. There were several windows on the property, but most of them were smashed or had gaping holes through them, like someone had thrown a very large rock through and no one had thought to fix it. It looked derelict; there was nothing around for miles up there, and it was a fair descent down into the creepy town. There were some dead trees that surrounded the house, but they didn't bring much protection or comfort because they were bare, and you could see right past them. One thing that they had noticed since being in this new world was that there was no weather, no warm or cold air at all. Were they even breathing? If so, what air were they breathing in and what was in it? The four of them walked up the steps and onto the porch, placing their feet carefully as they went so they did not fall through. The witch stopped and began chanting something to the house. All of a sudden, everything on the front of the house started to change colour; instead of being black and damaged, it was changing into a beautiful bright blue house with white trimmings on the outside of the windows and doors. She was using magic to put this place back together for the children; the floorboards underneath their feet were fully replenished, no falling through to hell for them. Once she had finished chanting her magic spell, she opened the brand new furnished door and they were welcomed by the darkness that was originally on the outside. It looked like there had been a fire in there. The constructions in the building had all collapsed in on themselves, and they were scarred with black ash. The air in the house was tight when they took a breath, and it felt like they were inhaling the fumes. Caleb put his hand to his chest in an attempt to breathe better, but he doubled over and began to cough violently. He ran out of the house quickly before he passed out from coughing too hard; he stayed there until he felt some relief. Back in the house, the witch began working her magic. After a whole five minutes, the house was back in working order. The walls were painted a white colour; each room on the bottom floor was varnished with different shaped furniture. One room was a library, filled with all sorts of books, fiction, non fiction and even a bible, which Ebony found amusing since they were practically already in hell. As they walked through the rooms, she traced her fingers across everything she saw, leaving tiny traces of herself on everything in there, not a speck of dust could be seen. They were all making their way back to the stairs at the front of the house when Caleb came back in from outside. He closed the door and joined them as they scaled the stairs to see what the second floor had to offer. The stairs were bare, but they were painted black with grey on the sides, they were also very steep, and if they were normal human beings, they would have stopped at the top of the steps and collapsed in a heap. When they reached the landing, they could see four large rooms, two of which were bedrooms, big enough to fit two king-size beds. And, the other two rooms were bathrooms with a walk-in shower and sauna. They had never seen anything like it and it was all theirs, just the two of them alone in this big house. Both of the bedrooms were decorated in a dark red colour, and the beds were all Victorian-style with four board posts at each corner and a canopy covering the top. The windows in each room were covered with a lining that stopped the sunlight from penetrating. However, the sun wasn't out today, it looked like it was never out. From the second floor, you could only see the dead trees t around the house; the wooden floors were slippery because they had just been waxed. Once they had all had a look around the second floor, they climbed their way to the second flight of stairs that lead to the third floor. On this floor, there were no specific rooms; it was just one big open space with a giant TV stuck on the wall. On the far end of the room was a humongous piece of glass that acted as a window, big enough to see down onto the whole of the town below them and out into the open in front of them. The sky was red in front of them; it looked like a storm was brewing ahead of them, but how could that be if they never had any type of weather here? They stared out the window, mind blown that this was their new life, homesick for the life that they knew, but hopeful that they weren't so alone with their immortality; they were with their own kind of people and for once, they felt like they fit in. They were left to their own devices by Marcel and Dora; once they had been in their rooms, they both decided to freshen up. Caleb went into his own bathroom and began to take his clothes off, one item at a time. While he did this, he started to run the shower until it was piping hot – that's how he liked his showers. He stepped into the shower, and the water started running down his body, droplets falling gently on his face and into his open mouth. He wet his hair and began to run his fingers through his hair and over his face. He was facing the shower, and his eyes were closed when he felt something behind him. He wanted to turn around, but he couldn't do it quick enough; a cold hand touched his shoulder blade and gently made its way down his back to the top of his bottom. He then felt something kissing his back; every inch was being caressed by gentle soft lips. When the kissing reached the top of his back, he turned around and found himself looking at Ebony. She was also wet from the shower; they stared at each other for a long time, and then they both leaned in – ready to kiss one another. When their lips met, an explosion erupted within both of them. They collided in a hot, passionate moment, stroking every body part. Caleb picked her up so her legs were wrapped around him. He left the shower running behind them while he carried her into the bedroom.

Chapter 11

A FEW DAYS LATER...

It was early morning, and the two of them had settled into their new quarters well. There was an endless supply of blood in the fridge, and human food if they felt like that. They never went hungry, but they needed blood to survive. They had just been hanging around the house, but today the witch was coming around to see them. After they had breakfast, they heard a knock on the door. Caleb got up and answered it swiftly. He was greeted by Dora, the witch in a purple gown and a strange orange hat; a strange array of colours that strangely suited her. She walked in and said hello to Ebony who was sitting in the kitchen, and then she spoke to both of them directly.

"We need to start your training today; something is coming and we need you to be at your strongest. We don't know what we face, but all we know is that it is bad; we witches saw it in our crystal balls. My dear husband Marcel is going to teach you how to feed and kill correctly; the way you killed before was far too reckless and manic," uttered Dora.

"Wait. What's coming? Why do we need to be trained?" asked Caleb inquisitively.

"All will be revealed in time my child. You will be strong because you are a newborn – we can put you on the right path so you will be our strongest fighter" replied Dora.

When the witch stepped outside, they both went upstairs and found black catsuits on their beds, skin-tight. There were also carbon fibre gloves laid on top of them. They got their clothes on and their boots, and then they went downstairs and proceeded out of the doorway to where Dora was standing patiently waiting for them. Once they were already, they started marching towards the little town at the bottom of the hill. As they were walking down; they noticed something moving around in the sky, like a snake slithering in the grass. Caleb pointed it out and Dora's reaction scared him.

"Oh my God, it's happening sooner than I expected," she cried.

She turned to them and told them to run. While they were running, he had to struggle to stay up right; he kept tripping on the rocky terrain. Once they reached the town, they ran for the big building that was the town hall, and once they were safely inside, they stopped to catch their breath – sweat was pouring down their faces. They looked around at the inside of the town hall lined with mosaic ceilings and painted tiles on the walls; it looked much bigger on the inside than it did on the outside. there was also a cold feeling about it, like something was lurking in the dark shadows that lingered on the edges.

"What do we do now, how are we going to be trained?" asked Ebony with a tone of curiosity.

Just as she said this, Marcel bounded through the double doors and announced himself.

"Now. We must begin before it is too late. I am going to provide you with lunch, fresh lunch. I will show you how to stop at just the correct moment and how to correctly dispose of the body."

The body of a man appeared in front of them, and they were shocked to find that it was a real living human with a pulse running through him. Marcel beckoned them to come forward to where the body lay; he told them to feed like they normally would, biting and sucking from the neck one on each side and as they did this, he guided them. When they were nearly done, he told them to slowly release their fangs; he told them to use their fingers to apply pressure on the wounds to stop the bleeding, and then they licked the blood from off their fingers. They stood back up and looked at the limp lifeless body in front of them; their next step would usually be disposing of the body in a grizzly fashion, but Marcel told them to pick the body up and follow him. Caleb heaved the body up and threw it over his shoulder, and followed Marcel to the back of the hall. He opened a trap door in the floor and a set of stairs emerged leading down into a basement of some kind. It smelt damp and musty. It was pitch black as they were walking down the steps, wobbling on some and as they approached the bottom of them a sort of putrid smell was emerging. A light flickered on above them, and it was making a buzzing sound that seemed to irritate Marcel. As they walked into the middle of the basement floor, Caleb began to see more clearly; there appeared to be blood splattered up the wall and guts and brain matter splashing across the ceiling. The smell was so repulsive and strong that he could taste it in his mouth. As he moved forward slowly, he had to cover his mouth with his arm to prevent him from puking his guts up.

This must have been a slaughterhouse, it certainly smelt and looked like one. There was many different weapons of torture strung up on the wall on individual hooks, giant meat cleavers, chainsaws, butcher knives, and even a hacksaw, all covered in a dark brown-red colour.

"What is this place?" he asked in amazement.

"This is where we bring our dead, to burn," replied Marcel clearly.

"So why all the blood and guts if they get burnt?" asked Caleb.

"We didn't always burn them. We learnt that over time, burning was the most effective."

He walked around the room until he reached an old and dusty bookshelf. He pulled a red book on the second shelf, and the whole wall turned 180 degrees, opening a secret passage. This passage was lined with old mediaeval torches on the wall, and old stonework covered all four sides of the narrow walkway. He told Caleb to throw the body into the tunnel, and that is what he did; the body smacked the cold floor with a loud thud, and Caleb took a quick step back. Marcel lifted his arm up to reach one of the torches from the side of the wall and dropped the burning hot flame onto the corpse; the body ignited in the flame, and you could hear the flesh bubbling over the snap and crackle of the bones. The fire kept on burning bright until eventually, there was nothing left of the body apart from the charred ashes.

Chapter 12

They were joined in the hall by three more vampires; they looked like Marcel in a way, but it was clear that they were not as high up on the ladder as him. They had serious looks on their faces, and the one with long bleach blonde hair was looking Ebony up and down – this ticked off Caleb. The other two both had cropped dark hair and were incredibly muscular – they were going to train them to fight properly and defend the town and their species.

"These are my best fighters; they will teach you how to fight and defend so you will be prepared for whatever is coming for us," said Marcel.

First up was Caleb, the blonde vampire called Demetri had him on the floor in seconds. This is what it was like for the first five minutes of training until Caleb could work out that he could use his new speed to his advantage. In no time, he was throwing Demetri high into the air and punching the wind out of him. When he landed on the floor, he pounced on top of him and got him in a tight chokehold, and that is when Demetri began to tap the floor hard – he was struggling a lot.

"Bloody hell Marcel, where did you find this one, nearly killed me" cried Demetri.

"He is a newborn; they are always extremely powerful," replied Marcel.

Now it was Ebony's turn; she had been a vampire for much longer than Caleb and she was very powerful, but she was also wise. She knew everything that was going to happen before it happened. For instance, she knew when she was going to be attacked and from which side she was going to be hit – she knew when to jump at exactly the right time, and when to dive and slide under her enemy to avoid death. She didn't need much training, but once they were both done for the day, they were full of bruises and starting to feel fatigued. They all crouched to the ground, some sat down, and some even led down.

"We now have some insight on what's coming for us. Years ago, an ancient enemy surfaced – you've heard of the vampire versus werewolf problem. Well, this one was much scarier, heretics. Heretics are a mixture of vampire and witch, and they are some of the most powerful beings in this realm; for years, they have when trying to wipe out the species below them, normal witches and vampires, warlocks, werewolves, and the occasional kitsune. They got successful when they attacked an old Louisianan werewolf pack; they demolished the whole town in which they lived – there wasn't a single trace of them left. We think that they want to destroy everything that is weaker than them, so that they can take over the world. We aren't going to let that happen, so that is why we need every available source that we can get; Caleb and Ebony make a brilliant addition to our ranks, and we should welcome them as our own," Dora addressed everybody.

Once Dora had finished talking to everyone, they left the town hall and made their way over to a building on the far side of the little town square. They opened the door and followed everyone inside curiously; there was noise buzzing and bouncing off all the walls. People were chatting loudly and laughing hysterically with their friends – they were like them, vampires, children of the night, devil spawn, whatever you would like to call them. They belonged to a family now, a rather large dysfunctional one, but nevertheless they had found a safe place. They mixed and talked to the vampire in the room. It was strange, but every single face in the room was a face of pure beauty. Men with gentle soft hair and piercing eyes, muscular arms, and body and cheekbones for days. The women had long flowing hair and gorgeous faces, long elegant legs, and petite hands – some had their hair cut short in cute bobs and pixie cuts – they were equally as beautiful despite their appearance. Being a vampire made them attractive – even if they were attractive before, they were turned. Dora stood up at the front of the hall on a little stage and told them all what she told the group in the other building before they came into that room. It was silent in the hall; everyone was looking around at everyone with shocked looks on their faces. Once she had stopped talking and everyone had time to process the impending news, they were hearing – they left the hall and everyone went off to their accommodation. Caleb and Ebony started their steep hike up the hill to the new house they now lived in.

Chapter 13

It was another morning in the new place, they had gotten used to waking up and looking at the view just outside their windows. This morning, the sky looked a little darker than usual, like something was coming down fast on them. Caleb was in the kitchen, drinking some blood from an old blood bag when Ebony walked down the stairs in her new fighting clothes and her high boots. They talked for a few minutes and then decided to take a walk into town. Once they had set off, they immediately felt something strange was happening. The town square was filled with an assortment of different creatures. There were big hairy werewolves and muscly vampires, witches, and warlocks of all shapes and sizes. They were practising, throwing their fireballs at targets littered around in different nooks and crannies. When they got to town, they went to the armoury to gear up for the fight. They were passed a gold and silver shield for protection and a big dagger in a sheath with their personal initials on – C for Caleb and E for Ebony – and finally, they had a branded sword they could wear over their shoulders and pull out whenever they needed to kill their attackers. The biggest weapon of all was their strength and their teeth; their teeth alone could rip out someone's jugular resulting in complete decapitation. They were ready for battle, all of them. This fight could determine the future of their species – the rise or the fall of vampires. Everyone was looking up at the sky as it started to change Colour drastically. The sky was now turning pure black with a tinge of red in it; if you looked close enough, you could see things moving in the blackness, it was trippy. They stood and stared up until the black started to fall from the sky, like a shooting star fading in the sky – they realised that the black mass above them was the biggest clan of enemy fighters that any of them had ever seen; the heretics had come to kill them all. The ground erupted underneath their feet as they landed with a giant bang; these were some of the scariest looking creatures they had ever seen. They had blue stringy hair and long pointy noses with big warts on; underneath their skin, you could see their veins with disgusting orange blood pumping through. Their fingers were long and honey with claws like fingernails on the end. They were all dressed in old fashioned wear, white blouses and brown corsets pulled tight over them; they were a pale blue colour almost white, and their eyes were bulging out of their ugly faces, one that landed near Caleb had one eye missing; where the eyes should have been a pit of darkness, like the entrance to hell itself was sitting in its eye socket. When they opened their mouths, they had gaps in their white soggy gums where the teeth should have been/ Wrinkles covered every square inch of their faces. A horrible squeaking high pitch scream came from their mouths as they started to attack anything within their vicinity. Caleb drew his dagger and began slashing at a heretic in front of him, and when it reached out for him with its talons, he brought his dagger down into the creature and it evaporated as quickly as it appeared, in a mist of brown dust – gone back to hell. He moved around and began to kill more and more as they dropped. He lost sight of Ebony, but the only thing he could think about right now was killing and surviving. He had only just been turned into a vampire, and he hadn't seen all the perks of being immortal yet. He wanted to live and wanted to be with Ebony forever and have children with her, but for now, he had to stay alive.

Chapter 14

Ebony was running and jumping on any heretic, she could, grabbing them with her strong hands and ripping their heads from their necks. On the next heretic, she did a cartwheel and landed on its neck, popping its head off like a pea in a pod. She pulled out her sword and pushed it straight through the heart of a large heretic and watched as the blood poured out of its chest cavity. Then she pushed her hand into its chest and ripped its bleeding heart from it. She had bright orange blood all over her hands, but she didn't get the urge to taste it. It looked and smelt poisonous, and for once, she could control herself. She looked around, and all she could see was a battlefield, werewolves jumping into the fight full force, ripping things to shreds, and warlocks throwing fireballs at them. Witches using magic potions to change them into something else, something easier to kill. Vampires baring their teeth and bleeding then to death, using their sheer strength to tear them limb from limb. Blood splattered on the floor, and everyone was slipping over it. Bodies were flying all over the place. She caught someone in the corner of her eye being obliterated; it was hard to tell who was winning. They kept falling from the sky one by one until, eventually, they stopped coming. A lot of the werewolves were dead. This was because the heretics used their blood to kill them because their blood was poison; They squirted it on their fur and as it sunk into their bodies; it got into their bloodstream. She looked around as the crowds began to die down, and she saw Caleb waking slowly, almost staggering over the pile of bodies lining the floor. When they saw each other, they ran until they collided in a warm, gentle embrace – they were both alive. The remaining fighters came together and made a plan. They knew that there was a leader. If they got to the leader and killed it, then maybe they would stand a chance. Although they had stopped coming from the sky, they knew that there was more on the way; they had to locate the leader sooner rather than later. They all went their separate ways, still fighting the odd heretic that came their way, but ultimately, they were looking for someone who could be a leader. Once they had been looking for some time, they were starting to lose hope. But then, they saw something descending from the sky that didn't look like the other creatures that fell from the sky. He wore a suit much like Marcels, and his hair was in a quiff. However, when looking closely at his hair, you could see red horns, like devil horns. Was this the devil? Or was it the leader of the heretic army? When he landed, his face became more clear; he was beautiful in a sort of angelic way; he looked like an Angel with a twinge of darkness. When he spoke, his voice was gentle, but it was also booming.

"I am Balthazar, the Mephistopheles. I am here to wipe you all out so me, and my new race can rule the world."

He looked around at the group of fighters on the ground and focused in on Ebony. He seemed to be intrigued by her.

"You, come here. I want a closer look at you." He pointed at Ebony in a rude manner.

Ebony didn't move. She was paralysed with fear to the spot.

Suddenly he lifted his hand and whispered something. Ebony began to move forward without moving herself. He was chanting a spell. When she was right in front of him, he stared deep into her soul through her eyes. He touched her face gently and stroked her cheek with the back of his hand.

"You are the most beautiful undead I have ever seen," he said.

Caleb was frustrated. This was his girlfriend this creep was touching and calling beautiful. He had to do something, but for some reason he had no control over his body. He was looking at the others also stuck in the same position as him, and then back to Balthazar. He was furious by now.

"I will be back with my children, and we will destroy your world. I will be the ruler of the new age and you will be my wife. Tell me what your name is girl?" he asked Ebony.

"E...Ebony," she replied shakily.

"Ebony, how nice – you're mine now. I am going to take you back home with me and you will wed me."

In a flash, he grabbed her with his thick hands and within a few seconds, he was beaming up back into the sky with Ebony in his grasp. Just like that, everything was gone; the Mephistopheles, Ebony, and all the dead heretics' bodies were left on the floor. Caleb cried out.

"NO! Where has she been taken? We must go after her Marcel, please let me go." He cried.

Marcel made his way over to Caleb to calm him down; he wrapped him up in his arms and held him like a baby.

"Don't worry, we will go and find her; we will search all of the corners of this universe until we get her back, I promise," insisted Marcel.

Caleb fell to the ground, sobbing into Marcel's shoes. As soon as he had found his one true love and his place in the universe, he had lost everything. An anger raged within him, soaring through the blood in his veins, making his heartbeat at a highly dangerous speed. All that he needed to do now was focus on his rage and channel it into something productive. He would train night and day until he was able and ready to go after Balthazar and destroy him. In fact, smash him into smithereens so that there would be peace among all creatures. He needed to do this for himself, and for Ebony.

Chapter 15

When Ebony awoke, she was in a completely different universe. It was dark everywhere and she was shivering from the cold. It made her skin crawl when she realised that she was all alone with this creepy-looking man. There were screeching noises all around them, and from what she could see, she was hovering over a big black hole; was she on a planet? She couldn't see anything that looked remotely human, like a town or houses. She was ripped away from Caleb, and now she had a gaping hole in her heart where he should have been. She was thinking about him and wondering where he could be, and if he would ever find her again. She was petrified. This creature kept staring at her closely and touching her face, and the more she looked at him, the more she felt sick. Why did he want her? What did she possess that he wanted so much? She didn't know what was going to come, but she knew that whatever it was, it was going to be scary. All that she could do was sit and wait for her rescue, if it ever happened...

Made in the USA
Monee, IL
03 May 2026

49437841R00036